WALT DISNEY PRODUCTIONS
presents

Donald Duck's
Big Surprise

Random House  New York
Book Club Edition

First American Edition. Copyright © 1982 by The Walt Disney Company. All rights reserved under International and Pan-American Copyright Conventions. Published in the United States by Random House, Inc., New York, and simultaneously in Canada by Random House of Canada Limited, Toronto. Originally published in Denmark as ANDERS AND FAR EN LAERESTREG by Gutenberghus Gruppen, Copenhagen. ISBN: 0-394-85393-8 Manufactured in the United States of America

0   C D E F G H I J K

Mickey's lunch party was
over.

Goofy, Mickey, and Minnie
waved good-bye to Donald Duc

"Thanks for lunch, Mickey," called Donald.

"Why don't we have a picnic at the beach next time?" said Minnie.

"Great! Come over to my house on Sunday," said Donald. "We can drive to the beach in my car."

"Gosh, thanks!" said the others.

On Sunday, Goofy, Minnie, and Mickey
set out for Donald's house.

Each of them carried things for
the picnic.

"What a great day for the beach!"
said Mickey.

Donald was busy waxing his car.
"Here we are, ready for our picnic!"
said Mickey. "I brought an umbrella!"
"I brought a radio!" said Goofy.
"And I brought lunch," said Minnie.
"But I can't go on a picnic," said Donald.

"But you promised us!" said Mickey.

"Did I? Well, I guess I forgot about it,"
said Donald. "I have a date with Daisy.
We can have a picnic some other time."

"We will have to take a bus to the beach,"
said Minnie.

The three friends waved good-bye to Donald.
But Donald was busy polishing his car.
He did not wave back.

Soon Donald's car was clean and shiny.

"It is almost time for
my date with Daisy.
I must get cleaned up,"
said Donald.

He went into his house.

Donald washed his face...

brushed his hair...

and fixed his tie.

Then Donald
put on his hat.

"What a handsome fellow I am!" he said.

Donald hopped into his shiny car.

"Gee, it will be fun to take Daisy
for a drive!" he said.

Soon Donald was at Daisy's house.
"Hi, Daisy! Are you ready for the ride
I promised you?" called Donald.

But Daisy was busy playing croquet
with her cousin, Gander.

"Oh, Donald, you said
you would call me,"
said Daisy. "But you
never did. I thought
you forgot our date.
So I made other plans."

"Well, um…I guess I did forget to
call," said Donald.

"Come play croquet with us," said Daisy.

"No, thanks," said Donald.

And he drove away in his shiny car.
He felt very sad.

"What can I do now?" Donald thought.
A street sign caught his eye.
The sign gave him an idea.

"Mickey, Minnie, and Goofy are at the beach!" said Donald. "I will go to their picnic."

Donald felt happy again.

He parked his car at the beach lot and went to find his friends.

Donald looked around the beach.
Then he saw Mickey's beach umbrella.
"Hi, folks! It's me, Donald!" he called.

"Hi, Donald! You came to the beach after all!" said Mickey. "We were just going for a swim. Come join us!"

"Thanks, but I
el tired," said
onald. "I want to
st for a while."

Donald sat down.
His friends headed for the water.
"Have fun!" Donald called to them.

Then Donald spotted the picnic basket.
"Say, this lunch looks good!" he said.

"I'll just try a cookie,"
said Donald.

Then he tried
a sandwich or two.

Donald kept
eating.
Then he drank
some lemonade.

Soon Donald was full.
He decided to take a nap.

Goofy, Minnie, and Mickey came back
from their swim.

They were all very hungry.

"Wake up, Donald!" said Goofy.

"Time for our picnic lunch,"
said Mickey.

"Gee, I'm not
very hungry. I
think I will
go home now,"
Donald said.

And off Donald went.

"Look! Most of the cookies are gone!"
said Mickey.

"And no sandwiches
are left," said Minnie.

"And somebody ate
the grapes!" Goofy
said.

The picnic was over in five minutes.

"Donald is impossible!" said Mickey. "He eats our food and then runs off!"

"He didn't even offer to drive us home," said Minnie.

"And he ate all those grapes!" said Goofy.

Tired and hungry, the friends waited
for the bus again.

"Donald never thinks of other people,"
said Mickey.

"He forgets his promises," said Minnie.

"He eats too much," said Goofy.

"We will have to teach him a lesson,"
said Mickey.

Donald woke up the next morning in
a good mood.
It was his birthday!

He jumped out
of bed.

He put on his
best suit and hat.

"Happy birthday!" he said to himself.
"This is going to be a great day!"

Donald looked out the window.
"Goofy will be here soon with
the mail truck," he said. "Oh, boy!
I can hardly wait to get all my
presents and cards."

The mail truck came by right on time.

"I had better go
help Goofy," Donald
said. "His sack
will be heavy with
all those presents."

But the mail truck went past Donald's
house without stopping.

"Hey, wait!" called Donald. "Don't you
have any mail for me?"

"No, not today," said Goofy.
And he drove away.

"There must be
some mistake,"
thought Donald.
"I will go check
at the post office."

"I'm sorry," said the postmaster.
"But there is nothing today for D. Duck."

Donald felt awful.
"Why don't I have
any mail?" he said.
"It is my BIRTHDAY!
I will go see Mickey
and remind him."

Mickey was busy in his garden.
He did not even look up.
"I can't talk now," he said to Donald.
"Come by some other time."

"Well, Daisy is sure
to remember my birthda[y]"
Donald said.

He ran to her house.

"Guess what day this is!" Donald said.
But Daisy did not even turn around.
"I am very busy now, Donald," she said.

Donald walked sadly around the town.
Why had no one remembered his birthday?
He felt terrible all day.
When evening came, he could see people
talking and laughing in their houses.
    "Everybody is having a good time,"
Donald thought. "Except for me. I might
as well go home."

Donald's house
looked dark and sad.

Donald slowly
walked up
the steps to
his front door.

He pushed the door open.

Suddenly the lights
went on!
The room was full
of people!

"Surprise! Happy birthday, Donald!"
everyone shouted.

They all had presents for him.

"Gee, I thought everyone forgot
my birthday," Donald said.

He felt very shy.

"We didn't forget," Minnie said quietly.
"But you forgot US at the beach yesterday.
We wanted to show you how it felt."

Donald hung his head.
"I'm really sorry, folks," he said.

"Well, we love you anyway," Mickey said.
"Even if you are sometimes…"
"IMPOSSIBLE!" everyone shouted.
"But happy birthday to you!"